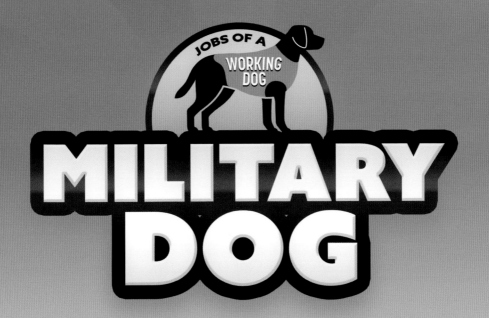

A Crabtree Branches Book

B. Keith Davidson

CRABTREE
Publishing Company
www.crabtreebooks.com

School-to-Home Support for Caregivers and Teachers

This high-interest book is designed to motivate striving students with engaging topics while building fluency, vocabulary, and an interest in reading. Here are a few questions and activities to help the reader build upon his or her comprehension skills.

Before Reading:

- *What do I think this book is about?*
- *What do I know about this topic?*
- *What do I want to learn about this topic?*
- *Why am I reading this book?*

During Reading:

- *I wonder why...*
- *I'm curious to know...*
- *How is this like something I already know?*
- *What have I learned so far?*

After Reading:

- *What was the author trying to teach me?*
- *What are some details?*
- *How did the photographs and captions help me understand more?*
- *Read the book again and look for the vocabulary words.*
- *What questions do I still have?*

Extension Activities:

- *What was your favorite part of the book? Write a paragraph on it.*
- *Draw a picture of your favorite thing you learned from the book.*

TABLE OF CONTENTS

A Brief History of Military Dogs

Dogs have served in human armies for thousands of years. Ancient Egyptians, Greeks, and Romans used attack dogs in battle, and guard dogs to watch over their camps.

The ancient Assyrians used war dogs to attack enemy soldiers.

Dogs have been used in battle as early as 600 B.C. when Alyattes of Lydia unleashed his war dogs on the Cimmerians.

 Attila the Hun used military dogs during his wars across the Roman Empire from 434 to 453 B.C.

Modern Military Dogs

Now called military working dogs, military dogs serve as **detection**, **scout**, and **patrol** dogs. Patrol dogs guard bases, airfields, and prisons.

Military working dogs detect threats that human eyes and noses cannot find. They are also walked around and put on full display to discourage attacks. Enemies don't want to mess with these dogs.

 **FACT**

There are memorials honoring military dogs all through the United States.

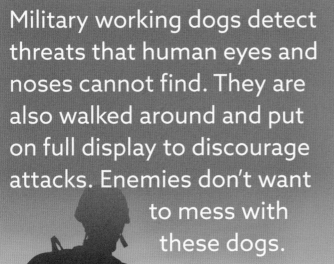

Detection Dogs

Bomb-sniffing dogs have been used in Iraq and Afghanistan. These dogs have found countless **improvised explosive devices (IEDs)**. This allows **demolitions** teams to defuse, or disable, the bombs. These dogs also find landmines and other hidden threats.

DANGER
DO NOT ENTER
EXPLOSIVE DETECTOR
DOG TRAINING
IN PROGRESS

FACT

Detection dogs can smell an explosive device inside of a car from up to 50 feet (15.24 meters) away.

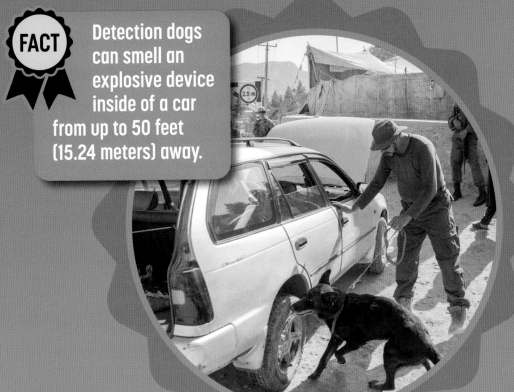

Scouting Dogs

A scouting dog goes with a team and tries to help them spot dangers before they become problems.

The dog will enter a building before the soldiers do. The dog will be wearing a **Kevlar** vest and cameras. The team will use the information the dog gathers to plan their attack.

 Scouting dogs are given radio ear pieces so their handlers can give them commands when they enter buildings on their own.

Breeds

Ancient armies wanted the biggest dogs that they could find. Mastiffs are some of the world's biggest dogs.

They were used not just for their power, but for their loud bark. The barks intimidated the soldiers on the other side.

 Zorba, an English Mastiff, was over 8 feet (2.4 meters) long and weighed 343 pounds (156 kilograms).

German shepherds have been the most popular dog of war for the last century. Labrador and golden retrievers are also popular choices.

These dogs have the size, speed, and intelligence necessary to help soldiers perform their tasks.

 FACT In 1899, Captain Max Von Stephanitz began to breed dogs to create the perfect military dog. The breed he created is known as the German shepherd.

Belgian Malinois and Dutch shepherds are cousins of the German shepherd. They're becoming more popular as military dogs. They are smaller, quicker, and just as smart as their larger cousins.

 Malinois, which is pronounced Ma-lin-wa, refers to the city of Maline, Belgium. This is the birthplace of the Belgian Malinois.

Picking the Perfect Puppy

The perfect puppy for a military job is one that listens. It needs size and speed, but more than anything it needs to obey its handler.

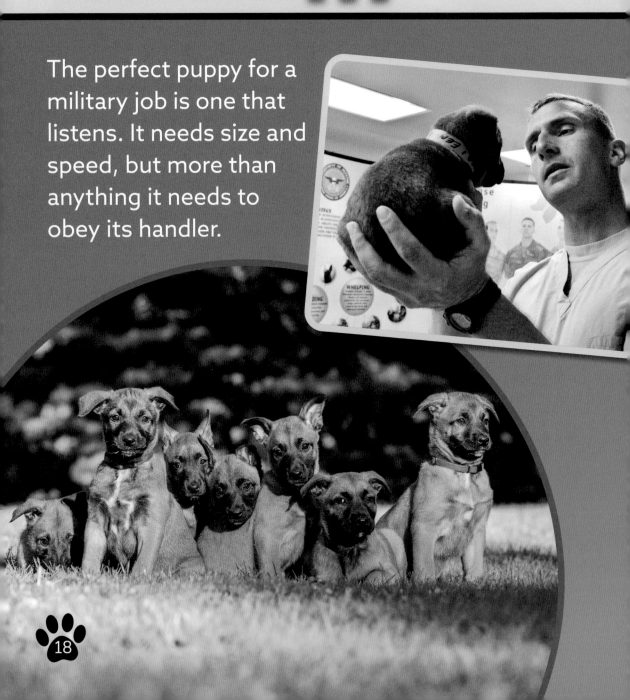

If a dog refuses to do something, lives could be lost. Just like human troops, dog soldiers must follow orders.

 **FACT** A fully trained bomb detection dog is valued at $150,000.

Training

Military dogs have to train for different jobs. One of the biggest challenges in training is getting the dogs ready for the sights and sounds of a battlefield.

A dog can know how to perform a task in training, but doing so can be much harder under pressure.

U.S. military dogs are trained at the Lackland Air Force Base in San Antonio, Texas.

Many military locations or targets cannot be reached by land. Military dogs have to learn how to travel by water and air to reach their intended locations.

Military dogs must also learn how to wear different types of gear. This includes body armor, goggles, oxygen masks, and harnesses.

Training for a military dog never really ends. Its basic training is 8 to 12 weeks long, depending on its army's rules. However it will continue to train every day until it is **deployed**.

 Some tactical vests worn by U.S. military dogs cost as much as $30,000.

Thank You For Your Service

During World War I, dogs alerted soldiers to the presence of enemy soldiers. Some dogs were also used to detect poison gas. The dogs could smell the gas before it reached the trenches, giving soldiers a chance to put on their gas masks. Sometimes gas masks were given to dogs, too.

EVEN A DOG ENLISTS WHY NOT YOU ?

660 MARKET ST, SAN FRANCISCO Or any U.S. Army Recruiting Station

 **FACT** In World War I, mercy dogs were loaded up with medical equipment and sent out on the battlefield to find wounded soldiers.

When Navy Seals went after Osama Bin Laden in 2011, they sent in Seal Team 6 and their trusted Belgian Malinois, Cairo. He was wearing body armor and a camera to gather information about the building.

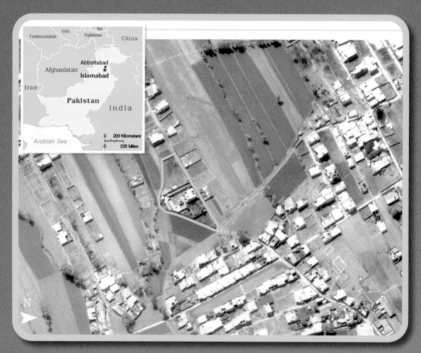

An aerial view of Bin Laden's compound in Pakistan.

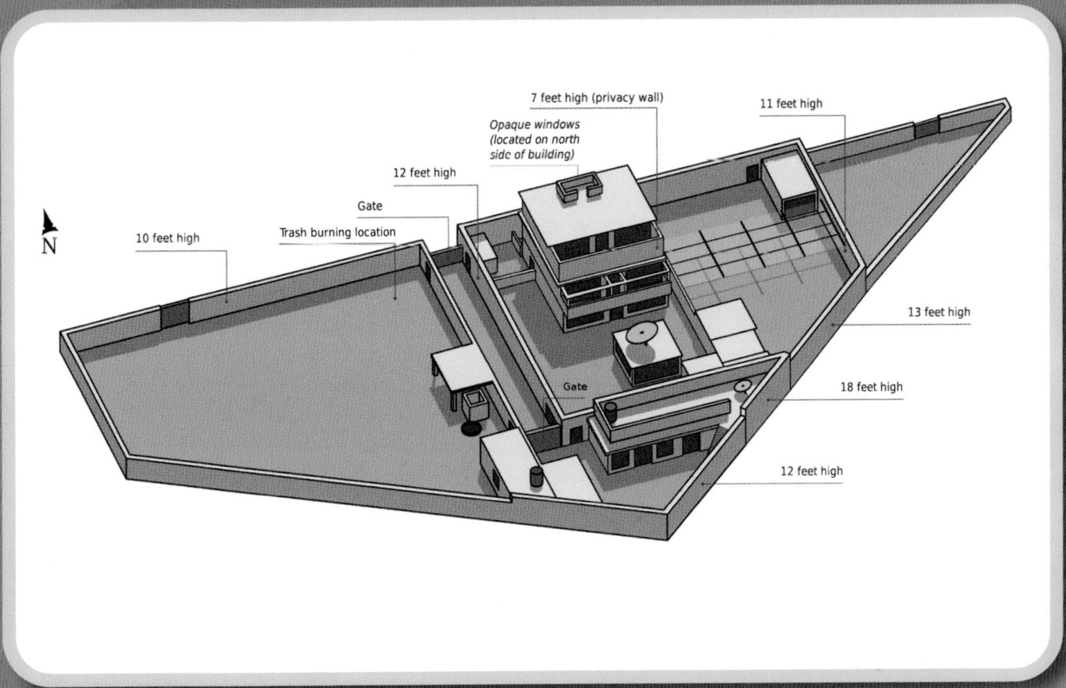
7 feet high (privacy wall)
11 feet high
Opaque windows
(located on north
side of building)
12 feet high
Gate
N
10 feet high
Trash burning location
13 feet high
Gate
18 feet high
12 feet high

According to one report, one of Cairo's many tasks was to help look for any hidden rooms or hidden doors in the compound.

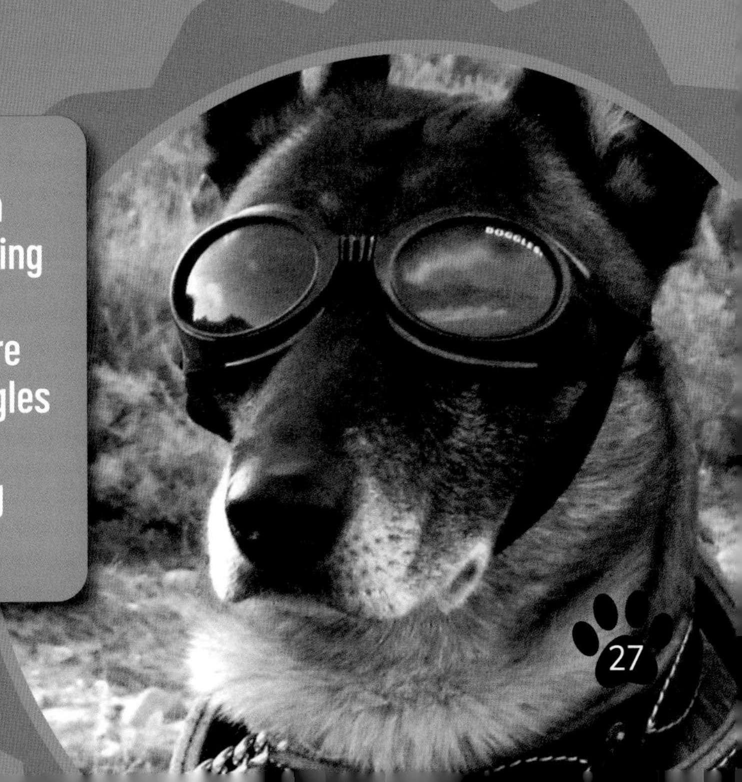

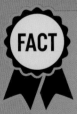

FACT

"Doggles" are sometimes worn by military working dogs like Cairo. Some doggles are heat-vision goggles that allow the dogs to see humans hiding behind walls.

Dogs have also been enlisted for use in space programs. Before people knew if it was safe for humans to go into space, they sent dogs aboard spacecrafts.

In 1957, Laika, a **mongrel** from the streets of Moscow, Russia, was the first animal to make an orbital spaceflight around Earth.

The Soviets launched 71 dogs into space. Unfortunately, 17 of them, including Laika, didn't make it back.

Laika wore this specially designed space suit aboard the Russian spacecraft Sputnik 2 in 1957.

Military working dogs are helping soldiers all over the world every day. The bond between a military working dog and its handler needs to be strong to make a successful team.

Glossary

deployed (di-PLOYED): a military term referring to sending troops to the places that they're needed

demolitions (dem-oh-LISH-uhnz): demolitions teams in the military defuse bombs safely so that people don't get hurt

detection (di-TECT-shuhn): the act of finding things that are hidden

improvised explosive devices (IM-pruh-vized ek-SPLOH-siv di-VISSEz): this term is used to describe homemade bombs that are set up as deadly traps

Kevlar (KEV-lar): a lightweight, bulletproof material used to protect soldiers and police officers

mongrel (MONG-gruhl): a dog of unknown, or unidentified, breed

patrol (puh-TROHL): keeping watch over a pre-determined area

scout (SKOWT): to scout is to go ahead of one's team and gather information

Index

Websites to Visit

https://www.mwdtsa.org/

https://myairmanmuseum.org/military-working-dogs/

https://www.akc.org/expert-advice/news/what-are-military-working-dogs/

About the Author

B. Keith Davidson

B. Keith Davidson grew up around dogs and has always been fascinated by the bonds that humans and these very special creatures share. Beagles are his favorite dogs, even if they are stubborn and frustrating. He has a Master's degree in Canadian History from Carleton University.

CRABTREE
Publishing Company

Written by: B. Keith Davidson
Designed by: Jennifer Dydyk
Edited by: Kelli Hicks
Proofreader: Janine Deschenes

Photographs: Cover: illustration of Dog(also on title page) © Nevada3, photo of soldier and dog © New Africa, helicopter © CC7, Page 4 Roman Camp © Massimo Todaro, dog © kavalenkava, Page 5 © Sammy33, Page 6 © PRESSLAB, Page 7 soldier and dog © Africa Studio, Page 12 © Ricantimages, Page 13 © Kachalkina Veronika, Page 18 (bottom photo) © DTeibe Photography, Page 28 © Shan_shan. All images from Shutterstock.com except Page 7 statue © Americasroof https://creativecommons.org/licenses/by-sa/3.0/deed.en, Pages 8, 9, 10, 11, 14, 15, 16, 17, 18 (top photo), 19, 20, 21, 22, 23, 27 (dog), 29 (dog with handler) courtesy of US Military, Pages 24, 25 courtesy of the Library of Congress, Page 26 and Page 27 (diagram) courtesy of US Government, Page 29 (top photo) James Duncan Flickr https://creativecommons.org/licenses/by-sa/2.0/

Library and Archives Canada Cataloguing in Publication

CIP available at Library and Archives Canada

Library of Congress Cataloging-in-Publication Data

CIP available at Library of Congress

Crabtree Publishing Company

www.crabtreebooks.com   1-800-387-7650

Copyright © 2022 **CRABTREE PUBLISHING COMPANY**   Printed in the U.S.A./CG20210915/012022

Published in the United States
Crabtree Publishing
347 Fifth Avenue, Suite 1402-145
New York, NY, 10016

Published in Canada
Crabtree Publishing
616 Welland Ave.
St. Catharines, Ontario L2M 5V6